Praise for Dr. Dave Ferruolo

"Absolutely enchanting! Girl in the Sun captures your heart from the first page with its vivid story-telling and unforgettable characters. Annie's adventure is a rollercoaster of emotions, filled with moments of joy, sorrow, and ultimately, hope. A must-read for anyone who loves stories that resonate with the beauty of overcoming adversity."

"Girl in the Sun resonated with me deeply. Annie's journey of self-discovery and resilience in the face of adversity is portrayed with such authenticity that it's hard not to feel connected to her story. Highly recommend for anyone looking for a story that's really inspiring."

"If you're looking for a story that feels like a warm hug, this is it."

"An exemplary narrative that delves into the intricacies of human emotions and the resilience required to face life's challenges. The author masterfully portrays the transformative power of love and connection, set against a backdrop that beautifully integrates the natural world."

# About Dr. Dave Ferruolo

With decades of unparalleled adventures and a profound understanding of the human experience, Dr. Dave invites you to explore a world where extraordinary encounters captivating stories. His unique blend of expertise in psychology and personal achievement, along with a wealth of diverse experiences, converges to create narratives that are nothing short of exceptional.

From daring exploits as a Navy SEAL to the depths of martial arts mastery, scuba diving in uncharted waters to scaling the heights of rock climbing, Dr. Dave's life has been a canvas painted with the vibrant colors of diverse experiences. These experiences form the foundation of his storytelling, infusing each word with authenticity and a deep connection to the human spirit.

Peering into the intricacies of the human psyche, Dr. Dave's work is a reflection of his profound comprehension of human nature. With roots in psychology and a lifelong dedication to understanding the human condition, he crafts narratives that resonate on a visceral level, inviting readers to explore the depths of their own humanity.

drdavebooks.com

# Girl in the Sun

# Girl in the Sun

Dr. Dave Ferruolo

Dr. Dave Books

Dr. Dave Books
PO Box 6421
Laconia, NH 03247
drdavebooks.com

Cover Artistry by SummerAnn Walker
(*SunshineArtistry.online*)
Cover design by Dr. Dave Ferruolo and Kozakura

ISBN: 9780977641284 (paperback)



Printed in the United States of America
0 1 2 3 4 5 6 7 8 9

First Printing, 2024

# Contents

# A New Beginning

The morning sun cast a golden hue over the small, sleepy town as Annie sat quietly in the back of the taxi. Her small hands clutched her only possession, a tattered brown suitcase. The driver, observing her in the rearview mirror, noted the subtle interplay of emotions on her young face.

"Everything alright back there?" he inquired, his voice tinged with a gentle concern.

Annie's gaze, distant and reflective, momentarily met his in the mirror. Her eyes, deep pools of brown, seemed to hold layers of unspoken stories.

They were slightly red-rimmed, the remnants of recent tears lingering like dewdrops. Her lips, a pale pink, trembled ever so slightly as she attempted a brave smile. "Yes, thank you," she replied, her voice barely a whisper, like a secret shared with the morning breeze.

She was garbed in a blue dress, its fabric faded, hanging loosely on her slender frame. A rich chestnut hue of hair cascaded in gentle waves around her shoulders, giving her an ethereal quality—a stark contrast to the sorrow that seemed to envelop her like a delicate shroud.

Sensing the depth of her emotions, the driver offered a nod of understanding and returned his focus to the road ahead. "You heading to your grandfather's, right? Must be nice, reuniting after so long."

Annie turned her gaze to the passing scenery, the sway of the trees outside mirroring the turmoil within her. "Yes, it's been a while," she murmured, her voice trailing off as she lost herself in the dance of the leaves.

The taxi stopped in front of a quaint house, its presence familiar and alien to Annie. She stepped out, her dress catching a light breeze, making it flutter around her like a soft embrace. The morning air was crisp and scented with pine and earth and seemed to pause around her as if acknowledging her presence. She stood momentarily, taking in the sight of the old house, its white paint peeling in places, revealing the stories of years gone by. The garden, though overgrown, was alive with the buzz of bees and the flutter of birds.

A tall figure appeared in the doorway, with a posture disciplined by years in the military. His expression was stern; his eyes, a deep blue, held a softness in them as they fell on Annie. "Welcome, Annie," he said, his voice gruff yet tinged with something that sounded like relief.

Annie hesitated, her feet rooted to the spot. The weight of her suitcase felt insignificant compared to the heaviness in her heart. She mustered a small smile, "Thank you, Grandpa." Her voice was soft, vanishing in the chorus of morning birds.

The house's interior was like a time capsule, filled with memories Annie could only vaguely recall. Old photographs adorned the walls, each telling a story of a time long past. Her eyes lingered on a picture of her mother as a child, her smile as bright and hopeful as the sun outside.

Her grandfather cleared his throat, breaking the silence. "I'll show you to your room," he said, leading the way up the creaky stairs. The house groaned under their steps as if awakening from a long slumber.

Annie's room was at the end of the hallway, a cozy space with a window overlooking the garden. The walls were painted a soft blue, and a small desk sat under the window, bathed in sunlight. It felt welcoming, yet the emptiness echoed loudly in Annie's mind.

"I thought you might like to be near the garden," her grandfather explained, placing her suitcase beside the bed. "Your grandmother loved to watch the sunrise from here."

Annie nodded, her gaze fixed on the garden. "It's beautiful," she said, her voice a mix of awe and sorrow. She imagined her grandmother sitting by this very window, her eyes reflecting the beauty of the dawn.

After her grandfather left, Annie remained by the window, her gaze wandering across every detail of her new sanctuary. The walls, swathed in a peaceful shade of blue, whispered of tranquil skies just after dawn. Her fingertips traced the textured brush strokes, each a silent bearer of untold stories.

Her attention was captured by the small desk beneath the window, a charming piece worn by time, each scuff and mark narrating tales of days long past. Atop it lay an old-fashioned ink pen and an untouched notebook, their presence inviting Annie to pour her innermost thoughts onto the blank pages. She could almost picture her grandmother there, pen in hand, perhaps finding solace in the words she penned.

Outside, the garden sprawled like a living tapestry, vibrant and untamed. Rich in color, roses reached towards the sun's warmth with a sense of yearning. The majestic and enduring trees surrounded the garden, their leaves rustling with secrets carried by the breeze.

A robin landed on the windowsill; head cocked curiously as it regarded Annie. Its feathers, bright against the weathered wood, shimmered in the sunlight. Annie watched, enchanted, as the bird hopped about before it took flight, its wings painting strokes of freedom against the sky's vast canvas.

As the robin prepared to take off, it paused and looked directly at Annie. In that brief, startling moment, she heard a clear, gentle whisper, "Everything will be okay, Annie." The voice seemed to come from nowhere and everywhere, startling her. She blinked, shaking her head slightly, dismissing it as a trick of her imagination, a fleeting echo of her thoughts. She watched as the bird disappeared through the densely leaved branches of a large oak tree.

The sun, climbing higher, cast its golden light into the room, creating a dance of shadows on the floor. It bathed Annie's face in warmth, a silent reminder of the world's enduring beauty amidst her turmoil. The dust motes in the air danced in the sunbeam, each a tiny testament to the life that had ebbed and flowed in this space.

Turning away from the window, Annie's eyes fell upon a small, framed photograph on the nightstand. It depicted her mother as a young girl, her smile as radiant and hopeful as the summer sun. Annie's heart ached as she picked it up, feeling the cool glass against her fingers. Her mother's eyes, mirrors of Annie's own, seemed to look back at her, bridging time and memory.

The room, with its simple furnishings and view of the vibrant garden, was a cocoon, enveloping

Annie in a new and achingly familiar world. It whispered tales of laughter and tears, of shared moments and solitude endured. Sitting there, amidst the remnants of her family's history, Annie felt a tentative connection to this place, a thread of belonging that, though frayed, still held the promise of comfort and understanding.

As Annie gently placed the photograph back, her eyes lingered once more on the garden, her thoughts a blend of sadness and wonder. The morning unfolded in this quiet contemplation, an unspoken dialogue between Annie and the room that was now hers, each observing and learning from the other in a dance of silent understanding. The robin's mysterious message lingered in her mind, an enigmatic whisper of things yet to come.

The rest of the morning passed in a quiet routine. Her grandfather busied himself in the kitchen, preparing a simple breakfast of scrambled eggs and toast. Annie sat at the table, the unfamiliar sounds and smells of the house enveloping her.

They ate in a shared silence, clinking cutlery against plates the only sounds filling the air. Annie's grandfather attempted small talk, asking about her journey, but the words felt forced, struggling to bridge the gap that time and distance had created.

After breakfast, Annie wandered into the garden, drawn to the wild beauty that thrived in neglect. The overgrown roses brushed against her legs, their thorns leaving gentle reminders of their presence. The garden was a living landscape of greens and browns, dotted with splashes of color from wildflowers that had found their way through the cracks.

She found a spot under the old oak tree, its branches reaching out like protective arms. The sun filtered through the leaves, casting patterns on the ground. Annie closed her eyes, letting the warmth seep into her skin and deeper into her bones.

At that moment, under the sun's watchful eye, Annie felt a sense of peace. It was fleeting, like the flutter of a bird's wings, but it was there. With its untamed beauty, the garden whispered promises of solace and healing.

As the day wore on, Annie's grandfather joined her in the garden. He moved slowly. His age evident in every step. He started pruning the roses, his hands skilled and sure. "They need a bit of care," he said, not looking up. "Just like us, I suppose."

Annie watched him work, the sun casting long shadows on the ground. She wanted to say something, to bridge the gap that stretched out between them, vast and silent. But the words remained unspoken, hovering like the bees over the roses.

The day faded into evening, and the garden was bathed in the soft glow of twilight. Annie and her grandfather sat on the porch, the creaky chairs offering a comforting rhythm. The air was cooler now, the pine and earth scents more pronounced.

In the silence, Annie thought of her parents, of the life she had lost. The pain was a relentless friend, a shadow that followed her every step. But here, in this garden, in the presence of the grandfather she barely knew, she felt the first stirrings of something new.

It was a beginning, fragile and uncertain, but a beginning nonetheless. In the embrace of the garden, under the sun's watchful eye, Annie dared to hope that maybe, just maybe, she could find her way through the darkness.

As night fell, the stars began to twinkle in the sky, a reminder of the vastness of the world, of the endless possibilities that lay hidden in the dark. Annie looked up, her heart filled with a quiet longing, a whisper of a dream just beginning to take shape.

# Unfamiliar Grounds

In the initial days at her grandfather's house, Annie found herself navigating a silent dance of awkwardness, each step tentative, as if walking through an unfamiliar dream. The house, a vessel of past lives and lingering memories enveloped her in an atmosphere steeped in history and emotion.

As she moved through the halls, the air held a hint of aged wood and a faint, comforting scent of lavender, reminiscent of a long-forgotten garden. The floorboards creaked under her feet, whispering secrets of the countless footsteps they had borne over the years. Each room she entered was like turning a page in a book of memories, the narrative of her grandfather's life unfolding around her.

The walls of the house were adorned with portraits, each frame a window into a bygone era. The most prominent among these were the portraits of her grandfather's wife. Her images were captured in the soft, golden light of yesteryears, her eyes sparkling with life and laughter that seemed to transcend time. Her smiling face, forever immortalized in paint and frame, was a poignant reminder of another profound loss, a presence deeply missed yet forever etched in the corners of the house.

In the living room, the furniture was arranged with meticulous care that spoke of her grandmother's touch. The armchairs were upholstered in faded floral fabric, the patterns worn smooth in places from years of use. A grand piano sat in one corner, its surface gleaming under the afternoon light filtering through lace curtains. Though untouched for years, the keys seemed to await the return of skilled fingers to bring forth melodies of a happier time.

Annie could almost smell the faint aroma of freshly brewed tea and baked cookies, a strong sensory memory that momentarily bridged the gap between past and present. She could picture her grandmother there, moving gracefully about the room, her laughter echoing off the walls, filling the space with warmth and vitality.

The dining room held a large oak table, its surface polished to a mirror-like sheen, reflecting the chandelier above. The chairs around it stood like silent sentinels, each one an observer of the countless meals and conversations that had taken place around them. The sideboard was laden with china and crystal. Each piece carefully arranged, a testament to her grandmother's attention to detail and love for hosting.

The aroma of aged spices lingered in the kitchen, mingling with the musty scent of old recipe books that lined the shelves. The kitchen was a mosaic of time, with modern appliances alongside vintage cookware. It was a place where past and present co-existed, a culinary heart of the home that held the essence of family gatherings and quiet mornings.

As Annie wandered through the house, each room and object seemed to whisper stories of her grandparents' life together - stories of love, joy, and the inevitable passage of time. In this house, memories clung to the walls like ivy, painting a vivid picture of a life rich in emotion and history.

This dance through the echoes of the past was a poignant journey for Annie. With its blend of nostalgia and loss, the house became a bittersweet backdrop to her new life. It was a museum of her grandfather's past, a sanctuary of memories, where every nook and corner held the remnants of a life lived with love and now remembered with quiet reverence.

Amidst this house of memories, Annie discovered solace in the garden, basking in the sun's comforting embrace. It was there, surrounded by whispering trees and the cheerful symphony of chirping birds, that she felt closest to her parents. With its overgrown beauty and tranquil ambiance, the garden became her sanctuary, a haven where the world's noise dwindled into a hushed murmur.

As Annie sat soaking in the gentle sun, flickers of memories began to weave through her mind. She remembered her mother's laughter, a sound as warm and embracing as the sunlight filtering through the leaves. Her father's strong, gentle hands, which once held hers as they explored the wonders of their backyard, now seemed to rustle in the leaves around her.

These memories brought both comfort and a deep ache. Her parents, so full of life and love, had been her entire world. Her father, an airplane mechanic, had always been fascinated by the skies. He would point to the airplanes he worked on and tell young Annie stories of distant lands and adventures that awaited in the clouds. Her mother, a schoolteacher, had a way of making the most superficial stories come alive, filling Annie's world with magic and wonder.

But their world had changed when they moved far away so her father could work at a bustling airport. The memories of her grandfather were sparse from those days, mere flickers of holidays and brief visits, his presence a distant but steady beacon in her early childhood.

The day that irrevocably changed Annie's life dawned like any other, yet it harbored an unforeseen storm that would leave permanent scars. They were aloft in her dad's Cessna 172, an older model that bore the signs of his meticulous care and attention. Her father, ever the vigilant guardian of their safety, seemed unconcerned by the brewing clouds on the horizon, his confidence in his abilities and his aircraft unwavering.

As they ascended, the world below shrank into a patchwork of multiple colors, a miniature version of their vast, beautiful world. Annie's heart danced with the thrill of flight, her eyes wide with wonder as she gazed out of the small window. Sitting in the co-pilot seat, her mother offered reassuring smiles as she continually turned to meet Annie's eyes.

But tranquility was short-lived. Dark, ominous clouds gathered with a sudden ferocity, engulfing the plane in a tempestuous embrace. The first jolt of turbulence hit like a rogue wave, sending a jarring shiver through the aircraft. Annie's stomach lurched, her heart pounding in her chest as the world outside the window morphed into a churning abyss of gray and black.

Her father's voice, usually a beacon of calm, carried an edge of concentration as he spoke into the headset, his hands moving with practiced precision over the controls. "It's okay. We're just hitting a bit of rough weather," he said, trying to mask the strain in his voice. The plane dipped and swayed, each movement more violent than the last, as if caught in a relentless sparring match with an invisible adversary.

The cacophony of the storm enveloped them.

Rain and sleet hammered against the fuselage, a relentless drumming that drowned out all other sounds. The wind howled like a beast in anguish, its fury palpable in every shudder and groan of the plane. Lightning flashed, brief and terrifying, illuminating the cabin in a stark, eerie light.

Annie's hands clutched the edges of her seat, her knuckles white, her body tensed for what was to come. Fear coiled in her gut, a visceral, primal response to the chaos around her. Her mother's hand found hers, their fingers intertwining in a silent pact of love and shared terror.

Then, with a ferocity that defied understanding, the world turned upside down. The plane spiraled, a helpless leaf caught in the storm's wrath. Annie's screams were lost in the roar, her senses overwhelmed by the unyielding spinning, the deafening noise, the blinding fear.

The moment of impact was a cataclysmic release, a shattering of reality into a thousand fragmented pieces. The world exploded in a symphony of breaking metal and shattering glass, a crescendo of destruction that tore through the very fabric of their existence.

In that instant, time ceased to have meaning.

Annie was adrift in a void of confusion and terror, her mind unable to grasp the enormity of what was happening. Her father's presence, once a steadfast pillar of strength and love, was ripped away in a cruel twist of fate.

When the chaos finally subsided, the world was a different place. The storm had passed, leaving behind a wreckage of life and dreams. Her father was gone, taken by the skies he loved so dearly. Her mother, a silent figure amidst the debris, was trapped in a liminal space between life and death.

For Annie, the crash was more than a moment of terror; it was a fracture in her very being, a schism that separated her past from her uncertain future. The memories of that day were etched in her mind, a haunting collage of sights, sounds, and emotions that would forever color her perception of the world.

Annie's survival from the crash was nothing short of miraculous, yet it came at a profound cost. Her petite frame, shielded by the back seat, had been her inadvertent sanctuary amidst the chaos. However, the protection it offered was not without its toll. She sustained severe injuries - broken bones that ached with a deep, persistent throbbing and a head trauma that left her world spinning in a dizzying, disorienting haze. The concussion she suffered was severe, resulting in a traumatic brain injury (TBI), a silent harbinger of the extraordinary sensory gifts that were yet to awaken within her.

In the aftermath, the hospital became Annie's temporary refuge, a place of sterile white walls and hushed voices. She lay there in a room not far from where her mother, now a silent figure lost in a coma, fought her own battle for life. The beeping of machines and the soft, rhythmic whoosh of the ventilator were a constant backdrop to her thoughts, a soundtrack to her new reality.

Though small and battered, her body showed a resilience that belied her young age. Each day brought a new challenge, a new pain, and a step towards recovery. The casts that encased her limbs were both a prison and a promise of healing, a visual reminder of the fragility of life.

As Annie lay in her hospital bed, staring at the ceiling, memories of the crash invaded her mind in unguarded moments. The terror, the confusion, the overwhelming sense of loss - it all came rushing back, leaving her breathless and frightened. The vivid recollections of her father's last efforts to save them, the storm's fury, and the shattering impact haunted her waking hours and disturbed her fitful sleep.

Her small size, which had once made her feel insignificant in the world's vastness, had been her saving grace in the crash. Yet, as she lay there, healing and grieving, she couldn't help but feel a deep sense of solitude, a profound loneliness that seeped into her bones.

The emotional scars ran deeper than the physical ones. Annie had not only lost her father, her hero, and protector, but her mother too had been taken from her, albeit in a different way. She was there, yet unreachable, lost in a world where Annie could not follow. This duality of presence and absence was a constant ache in Annie's heart, a reminder of what had been and what could never be again.

As Annie gradually healed in the stark, antiseptic room, a part of her remained trapped in the wreckage of the plane in the storm-tossed skies that had claimed so much. Her journey through recovery was not just a physical one but an emotional and spiritual odyssey, leading her toward a future where pain and loss were interwoven with the awakening of something extraordinary within her.

Now, as she sat in her grandfather's garden, the memories enveloped her, both a soothing balm and a reminder of her loss. She could feel her parents' presence in the rustling leaves and hear their voices in the wind. The garden seemed to understand her grief with its untamed beauty, offering its quiet strength as she navigated through her sorrow.

In this unfamiliar place, surrounded by remnants of a life once lived, Annie began to find a semblance of peace. The garden, a testament to nature's enduring beauty, held her in its embrace, whispering to her of resilience and hope, even in the face of the most profound losses.

# The Flicker of Connection

One afternoon, Annie found solace under the old oak tree in her grandfather's garden, a place where time seemed to pause, and the world softened around her. The sunlight filtered through the leaves, dancing in dapples on the ground, creating a tapestry of light and shadow. As she sat there, the sun's rays caressed her skin with warmth and an inexplicable energy that seemed to reach deep within her, stirring something dormant.

Annie closed her eyes, letting the gentle warmth bathe her face. The light painted vibrant patterns on the inside of her eyelids, a kaleidoscope of oranges and reds that pulsed with each heart beat. It was in this serene solitude that something extraordinary began to unfurl within her.

With the sun's rays sifting through the oak tree leaves, Annie's mind began to wander. She felt an unusual connection, as if the sunlight was not just a physical warmth but a deeper, more profound touch, reaching into her very being.

Vivid images unfolded in her mind. She saw her parents' faces. Not just as still memories but alive and full of expression. Her father's eyes held a familiar spark, his smile almost bridging the gap between them. Her mother's laughter rang in her ears, a sound, a presence, wrapping Annie in comfort.

Intermingled with these images were fragments of conversations and time spent together. Her mother, reading stories at bedtime, filled the air with a sense of magic. Her father's laughter, hearty and joyous, reminded her of days of exploration and wonder.

But these memories weren't solely hers. Annie felt she was accessing something broader, a stream of consciousness where emotions and thoughts merged. Joy, sorrow, and a deep love flowed through her, feelings that seemed unfamiliar and intimately known.

The sunlight seemed to unlock a pathway to a realm beyond the physical. Annie felt part of something vast, a complex blend of human experiences, merging moments and emotions.

Time seemed to lose its linear nature. Past and present blended, and the distinction between her experiences and those of others blurred. She was in a realm where emotions and memories were vivid and alive, each a thread in the larger fabric of existence.

She felt a sense of unity, a realization that her existence was part of a larger, interconnected network. The sensation was profound, revealing a universe that was not distant but intimately connected with the life coursing through her.

This experience transcended mere imagination. It connected to a deeper truth, where the physical and spiritual realms intertwined, speaking a language that resonated with her heart and soul.

Enveloped by a sense of tranquility and connection, Annie felt a gentle and comforting presence. It felt like her mother's essence reaching out to her from the depths of her coma. As delicate as spider silk yet imbued with an almost tangible intensity, this connection enticed Annie to reach deeper within herself.

Annie extended her mind, trying to grasp this elusive thread. A vivid memory burst forth, a long-forgotten moment from her childhood. She was in the garden, a young child immersed in play. The sun filtered through the oak leaves, casting a kaleidoscope of light around her. Her laughter mingled with the rustling of the leaves, creating a symphony of innocent joy.

Her mother was there, her presence a soothing anchor in the vibrant landscape of the garden. Young Annie, caught in a moment of childlike wonder, had declared with a giggle that the tree was speaking to her. It seemed silly, fanciful, yet her mother responded with a knowing smile.

"Sometimes, that happens," her mother had said, her voice gentle yet serious. "We come from a long line of women who perceive the world differently. Sometimes, if the living essence of nature is comfortable, it communicates."

This revelation, shared in a moment of maternal bonding, had opened a world of wonder for young Annie. Guided by her mother, she had begun to explore this gift, this unique way of connecting with a world beyond. But this exploration was short-lived. They had moved to the city soon after. The noise and chaos of urban life had severed the blossoming connection. Annie realized now that such a connection could only flourish in the quiet, peaceful space of undisturbed nature.

Memories resurfaced after years of being tucked away in the recesses of her mind. They brought a new understanding. Annie realized that her mother had recognized and nurtured this gift in her from an early age. The garden, with its whispering trees and sun-dappled tranquility, was not just a place of refuge but a generational gateway to rediscovering this lost part of herself.

Amid her newfound realization, Annie's thoughts turned to the very garden she sat, a place deeply intertwined with her family's history. This sacred ground had been part of her lineage since the mid-1600s, its roots entangled with tales as old as time. Family lore spoke of ancestors from the Plymouth Colony, individuals who had grown weary of the rigid Puritanism of the English Separatist Church. Seeking a life more attuned to the natural world and indigenous values, they ventured north, eventually settling along the rugged coast of Maine, where they founded a community that echoed the harmonious philosophies of the native tribes.

Among these ancestors was one of Annie's forefathers, a man whose heart was captivated by the love of a young Penobscot woman. She was not just any woman but the daughter of the tribe's elder, a connection that symbolized a deep bond between the two cultures. In a gesture of unity and respect, her grandfather, the tribe elder, bestowed this land upon the newlywed couple as a gift. It was a sacred trust, a symbol of their union and the merging of two worlds.

Over the centuries, this land had been zealously protected, governed by covenants that ensured it would never be sold, always passed down through the maternal line. It was a testament to the reverence and respect her ancestors held for the land and its history. The garden, with its ancient trees and untouched beauty, was not just a piece of land; it was a legacy, a guardian of stories and traditions, an emblem of a deep, spiritual connection to nature and the past.

As Annie absorbed the weight of this history, she felt an even deeper connection to the garden and the ancient oak under which she sat. It was as if the land itself was part of her, a living entity waiting for her, calling her to rediscover the gift she had unknowingly inherited. In this hallowed space, it was here that the whispers of the past and the songs of nature intertwined, creating a symphony that resonated with the essence of her being.

With this profound understanding, Annie felt a renewed sense of purpose. The sacred garden was not just a refuge but a gateway to a deeper understanding of herself and her place in the continuum of her family's history. As the sun descended, casting long shadows across the verdant landscape, Annie opened her eyes, viewing the world around her with a newfound clarity. The garden, steeped in history and spiritual significance, had awakened something within her, guiding her on a path of discovery and connection with the living spirit of nature.

This awakening marked the beginning of Annie's journey into the depths of her abilities. It was a path lined with the light of discovery and the shadows of uncertainty, but Annie sensed it was a path she was meant to tread. In the heart of the garden, under the watchful eye of the sun and the old oak tree, Annie had found the first flicker of a connection that would guide her through the uncharted territories of her heart and mind.

Annie's grandfather had been watching her from the window, a knowing smile on his lips. He recognized the signs that he had seen in Annie's mother when she was a child playing in the garden. His wife, Annie's grandmother, had the same gift, a unique ability to connect with the world in a way most could not. It had been strong in her and even stronger in Annie's mother. But in Annie, it seemed magnified. Maybe the accident had played a part in reawakening or strengthening this dormant ability.

When Annie eventually rose from her place under the towering oak, there was a new light in her eyes. She walked back into the house, carrying with her a fresh understanding of her gift and her connection to the garden and her family's history.

Her grandfather met her as she entered. His usual aura of reclusiveness and sorrow visibly softened. Watching Annie connect with her abilities had melted away some of the darkness that had enveloped him since his wife's passing. In Annie, he saw not only the passed-down essence of his beloved wife but also a promise of renewal and hope.

This moment formed a deeper bond between

Annie and her grandfather. As they stood there, a flicker of connection sparked between them, a silent acknowledgment of their shared loss, understanding, and the unspoken recognition of Annie's gift. It was a significant step in healing the wounds of the past and building a new relationship in the present. For her grandfather, Annie's arrival and awakening had rekindled a part of him he thought lost. For Annie, her grandfather was no longer just a figure from her past but a needed part of her journey forward. Together, they began navigating the complexities of their shared history, grief, and the extraordinary path ahead for Annie.

# Echoes of Past and Future

As time passed, Annie's communion with the ethereal sense intensified. The whispers of the wind and the sun's tales became clearer, more coherent, as if they were speaking directly to her soul. During these quiet moments in the garden, under the benevolent gaze of the sun, Annie felt an indescribable closeness to her mother. She envisioned her lying in the hospital bed, adrift in a realm between consciousness and oblivion.

Each day, Annie would sit beneath the old oak tree, its ancient branches like arms of comfort encircling her. She spoke to her mother through the veil that separated them. Her words, imbued with longing and love, recounted the details of her new life with her grandfather. She described the sunrise, the rustle of the leaves, the vibrant hues of the flowers – all in the hope that these vivid descriptions would serve as a beacon, guiding her mother back to the world of the living.

Perched at the crest of the rolling hills along the Penobscot River in Maine, the oak stood as a guardian of time and memory. Its massive trunk, a testament to decades weathered and witnessed, boasted contours and curves that had naturally formed into cozy seats. It was as if the tree, through the essence of its growth, had intentionally sculpted these resting spots, inviting those who sought solace or connection.

From this vantage, Annie's view encompassed a breathtaking sweep of Maine landscapes. To the south, the scene opened to glimmers of the distant Penobscot Bay and the intricate waterways of the Mt. Desert Narrows, a labyrinth of bays weaving through the coastline. Further towards the southeast, the expanse of the Atlantic Ocean stretched into the horizon, its vast waters merging with the sky. On clear days, Annie could clearly see the flickering dance of the sun's rays on the salted Atlantic waters.

The easterly view presented elusive glimpses of the Gulf of Maine and the distant sheen of the Bay of Fundy. Here, the morning sun emerged from the ocean's embrace, casting a radiant glow that heralded the start of a new day.

To the west, the landscape transformed into the untamed beauty of Maine's 100 Mile Wilderness, an expanse of forest, rivers, and lakes that whispered tales of the wild and untouched. This view, a panorama of dense, green wilderness, was a reminder of the enduring majesty and mystery of nature.

Seated in one of the tree's natural alcoves, Annie felt at the center of an extraordinary confluence of natural beauty. The diverse views offered a sense of expansive freedom and an intimate connection with the land. The oak, with its commanding presence and nurturing embrace, seemed to cradle her in a world both grand and deeply personal.

This sacred spot beneath the oak had become more than just a refuge; it was a gateway to profound understanding and a heightened sense of oneness with the world. The tree, with its encompassing views, stood as a guardian of her journey, offering Annie a place to commune with the natural elements, to listen to the earth's ancient rhythms, and to feel a deeper connection to the universe.

Here, under the oak tree, Annie found a haven of peace and belonging, a physical and spiritual anchor amidst the ever-shifting landscape of her life. The oak, with its panoramic embrace, stood as a living symbol of the beauty and enigma of the world, a steadfast companion in her journey of exploration and connection.

As time passed, Annie's communion with the ethereal sense intensified. The whispers of the wind and the sun's tales became clearer, more coherent, as if they were speaking directly to her soul. During these quiet moments in the garden under the benevolent gaze of the sun, Annie felt an indescribable closeness to her mother. She envisioned her lying in the hospital bed, adrift in a realm between consciousness and oblivion. And although the Boston hospital was over 250 miles away, her mother felt only a reach away.

In these serene hours, Annie would sit beneath the old oak tree, its ancient branches like arms of comfort encircling her. She spoke to her mother through the veil that separated them, her words imbued with longing and love. She recounted the details of her new life with her grandfather, describing the sunrise, the rustle of the leaves, and the vibrant hues of the flowers – all in the hope that these vivid descriptions would serve as a beacon, guiding her mother back to the world of the living.

Annie felt a connection with her father, during one unexpected experience. In a space that transcended time, they watched ethereal videos – memories of their past together. She relived their adventures and fun, each memory a vivid, joyful echo of their bond. As these visions faded, Annie felt an overwhelming sense of her father's presence, a comforting assurance that he was always with her.

On another day, as Annie sat enveloped in the tranquility of the garden, her senses attuned to the subtle rhythms of nature, she was drawn into a deeply vivid vision, a window into a future yet to unfold. It was as if time had peeled back its layers, offering her a glimpse into a tapestry of moments not yet woven.

In this vision, Annie saw herself, but not as she was now. She was older, her features etched with the grace and wisdom of passing years. There was an unmistakable aura of contentment about her, a serenity that spoke of a life well-lived. She was not alone; by her side was a young girl, her daughter, a radiant reflection of her own joy. The child's laughter was like music, a melody that resonated with the deepest chambers of Annie's heart. The bond between them was palpable, a visible thread of love and understanding that connected their souls.

The setting of this vision was a familiar yet transformed version of the garden. The oak tree, under which Annie now sat, stood taller, its branches wider, as if it too had matured alongside her. The flowers around them were in full bloom, creating a kaleidoscope of colors that painted the landscape with vibrancy and life.

In the periphery of this vivid tableau, there was a figure, a silent observer to this scene of familial bliss. It was an older woman, her features softened by time, cradling a newborn in her arms. This woman held the baby with a tenderness that was both protective and loving. There was something hauntingly familiar about her, a connection that tugged at the edges of Annie's consciousness.

Annie strained to recognize the woman, and a thought flickered through her mind – could this be her mother, somehow a part of this future vision? The woman's presence was enigmatic, shrouded in a gentle mystery of a future story still being written.

This vision, though fleeting, left an indelible impression on Annie. It was as if she had been granted a rare glimpse into a future filled with love, happiness, and the continuation of her family line. Yet, the presence of the older woman holding the newborn lingered in her thoughts, a sublime foreshadowing of possibilities and mysteries yet to be revealed.

As Annie emerged from the vision, the garden around her seemed more alive, pulsating with unseen energies and untold stories. The experience had not only given her a glimpse of a potential future but had also deepened her connection to the present, to the land, and to the legacy of her family. It was a reminder that the threads of her life were part of a larger story, one that spanned generations and held the promise of continuity and renewal.

In yet another sun-drenched afternoon under the oak tree, Annie found herself immersed in a conversation about her grandfather. As she spoke to the unseen presence of her mother, her words flowed with a blend of worry and wonder about the man who had become her guardian. During this ethereal exchange, insights and knowledge about her grandfather, beyond her own experiences, began to unfold within her, painting a vivid portrait of his life and character.

Her grandfather, a true son of Maine, had his roots deeply entrenched in the small community where his parents owned a quaint general store and gas station. He spent his childhood there, a time marked by the simplicity of small-town life and the warmth of a loving family. The store was not just a business but a community hub, and he, as a young boy, was part of its heartbeat, learning the values of hard work and community service.

At the age of seventeen, driven by a sense of duty and the desire to follow in the generational foot-steps of military service, he joined the Marines. His time in the service was transformative, a period that shaped him in profound ways. He saw combat in Vietnam, an experience that left indelible marks on his soul, the invisible wounds of war that he carried within him. Despite the hardships, he distinguished himself through acts of bravery, earning the Silver Star, a testament to his courage and selflessness.

After seven years of service, he returned home,

a changed man, to take over the family business. It was during this time that he met a local girl, a meeting that blossomed into love and eventually marriage. With their union, her family gifted them the ancestral land, the very land where the house, the beloved garden, and the ancient oak tree stood. This land, steeped in history and natural beauty, became the foundation of their new life together.

His wife, and later their daughter, became the anchors that pulled him back from the shadows of his war experiences. They brought light, joy, and purpose into his life, healing him in ways he never thought possible. Together, they built a life filled with happiness and contentment, their days echoing with laughter and love.

But this bliss was not to last forever. The distance of his daughter and granddaughter coupled with the passing of his wife plunged him back into an abyss of grief and solitude. The loss was a blow that dimmed the light he had found in his family, leaving him to navigate a world that suddenly seemed devoid of color and warmth.

As Annie delved deeper into these revelations, she began to see her grandfather not just as a stoic figure marked by loss, but as a man who had traversed vast landscapes of human experience. From the innocence of a small-town childhood to the horrors of war, from the joys of love and family to the depths of grief, his life was a novel of highs and lows, joy and sorrows.

This newfound understanding of her grandfather's journey infused Annie with empathy and a profound sense of connection. Even at her young age, she instinctually knew her presence might be the beacon he needed, a light to guide him back to a world where love and joy could flourish once again. This insight strengthened her resolve to reach out to him, to help heal the wounds of the past and to reignite the spark of hope and happiness in his life.

In this journey of discovery and connection, Annie found herself becoming not just a granddaughter but a vital link to her grandfather's return to a life filled with light and love. This ethereal dialogue seemed to encourage Annie to be patient and nurturing, to help guide her grandfather back to a state of love and happiness. It was as if her mother's spirit was guiding her, offering wisdom and support in this endeavor.

During these moments under the oak, Annie also felt a connection with her father. In a space that transcended time, they watched ethereal videos – memories of their past together. She relived their adventures and fun, each memory a vivid, joyful echo of their bond. As these visions faded, Annie felt an overwhelming sense of her father's presence, a comforting assurance that he was always with her.

This chapter in Annie's life marked significant emotional, psychological, and spiritual growth. The experiences under the oak tree were not just moments of connection but also of profound personal development. They set the stage for the next phase of her journey – building a deeper relationship with her grandfather, understanding the depths of her gift, and preparing for the complexities of the future.

The echoes of the past, the whispers of the present, and the glimpses of the future all converged under the oak tree, guiding Annie through a transformation that was both personal and transcendent. The journey ahead promised to be one of deeper exploration, of strengthening bonds, and of embracing the full potential of her extraordinary gift.

# Mending Bonds

As weeks transitioned into months, the bond between Annie and her grandfather transformed. They found themselves sharing meals and engaging in conversations about everyday things like the weather and the nuances of the garden. Their relationship deepened through shared adventures – exploring the mountains, wandering along the ocean shores, and trips to Boston to visit her mother. These experiences gradually strengthened their connection, turning simple moments into treasured memories and bridging the emotional distance with a growing sense of understanding and camaraderie.

On one such adventure, Annie's grandfather took her on a drive across Maine and through the White Mountains of New Hampshire. The destination was a secret; no matter the constant prodding, her grandfather would not tell.

Annie's first glimpse of the Mount Washington Hotel stirred a sense of awe. The grand structure, built over a century ago, stood majestically against the backdrop of the White Mountains. It was a place of fantasy, of dreams, Annie thought. As they wandered through the lobby and halls, each meticulously crafted detail spoke volumes of an era defined by its dedication to artistry and elegance. The grand architecture and sumptuous decor, a labor of love by skilled Italian artisans, reflected a profound commitment to excellence.

This reverence for detail and quality resonated with Annie, prompting reflections on her life and relationships. It dawned upon her that the same principles applied to her bond with her grandfather. Just as the artisans of the hotel had paid attention to the finest details, she realized the importance of nurturing the nuances of their relationship. It wasn't just about grand gestures but also about understanding the subtleties of each other's experiences and emotions.

Annie considered how pride in one's work and creations, like the hotel's timeless elegance, was akin to pride in one's family and personal connections. The care and attention devoted to building something beautiful and lasting could be mirrored in how she and her grandfather strengthened their bond. This subtle realization highlighted the importance of cherishing and cultivating their relationship with patience, care, and an eye for the delicate intricacies that make each interaction meaningful.

Through this introspection, Annie began to appreciate the deeper layers of her connection with her grandfather. Much like the grand hotel, their relationship required time, effort, and a keen eye for detail to develop its full potential and beauty.

As Annie and her grandfather stepped out into the verdant backyard of the Mount Washington Hotel, they were greeted by a breathtaking panorama. Expansive green fields gently merged into a dense forest, serving as a natural prelude to the majestic Presidential Mountain Range. Dominating this range was Mount Washington, its towering peak a formidable presence against the skyline.

Annie stood in awe, her gaze drawn to the summit, which stood as a sentinel overlooking the landscape. This sight marked a transition from the grandeur and history of the hotel to nature's raw, wild beauty. The sight of the mountain, so stark and powerful, stirred something within her, a sense of anticipation and excitement for what came next.

As the Mount Washington Cog Railway began its ascent, Annie felt a mix of exhilaration and trepidation. The historic train, a marvel of engineering, chugged upwards, its cogwheels engaging with the tracks in a rhythmic clatter. Each jolt and vibration of the train as it navigated the steep incline echoed through Annie's body, amplifying her sense of adventure.

Looking out the window, Annie was mesmerized by the changing landscape. The dense trees that had seemed so tall at the base now appeared to shrink as they ascended. The rough terrain unfolded before them, unveiling an expansive, rugged allure. The steep slopes of Mount Washington, covered in rock and sparse vegetation, seemed to defy the very possibility of ascent. Yet, here they were, slowly making their way up an impossible path.

Annie's mind wandered to the parallels between this journey and life itself. The railway's audacious climb up the rugged terrain of Mount Washington was a testament to human determination and ingenuity. It reminded her that perseverance and creativity could traverse even the most daunting paths. She thought about the challenges she faced in her own life, the steep slopes of grief, and the seemingly impassable obstacles. This journey symbolized that no matter how impossible a challenge might appear, there was always a way through – a path forward could be forged with willpower and innovative thinking.

As the cog railway continued its climb, the air grew cooler, and the landscape became more rugged and barren. The view from the train was breathtaking –mountains, valleys, rivers, all so small they could fit in her hand. It was a reminder of the vastness of the world and the slight but significant place one occupies within it. Upon reaching the summit, Annie emerged from the train into a world transformed. The grandeur of the landscape, with its sweeping views of the Northeast, instilled a profound sense of wonder and humility.

Annie felt a rush of emotions – awe at the vastness, pride in the journey taken, and a newfound appreciation for the resilience and determination it symbolized. Standing atop the highest peak in the Northeast, she realized that life's challenges, much like this rugged ascent, could be surmounted with perseverance and ingenuity. This moment was not just an achievement of reaching the summit; it was an enlightening ascent in understanding the potential within oneself to overcome even the steepest of life's challenges.

That evening, as Annie and her grandfather sat by the campfire, their conversation gently unraveled the day's events. The crackling fire cast a warm glow and the scent of toasted marshmallows mingled with the crisp mountain air.

"Grandpa, today felt like a journey through time," Annie mused, watching the flames dance. "The hotel was like stepping into the past, wasn't it?"

Her grandfather nodded, adding a log to the fire. "Yes, it's a reminder of how things were built to last back then, with care and pride in every detail."

Annie contemplated this, the embers glowing

brightly. "And the cog railway, climbing up so steeply – it's like life, isn't it? Sometimes, the path is difficult, but we keep going."

Her grandfather smiled, his eyes reflecting the firelight. "That's right. It's about the courage to face those steep climbs and the ingenuity to find a way up."

As they roasted marshmallows, their conversation ebbed and flowed. They spoke of small things – the stars, the whispering trees – and then delved into more profound reflections on life, courage, and the beauty of human endeavor.

"In every adventure, there's a lesson," Annie concluded, gazing at the starlit sky. "Not just about the world, but about ourselves too."

"Yes," her grandfather agreed, his voice soft with emotion. "And about how our journeys, no matter how difficult, shape who we are."

In the quiet of the mountain night, their bond deepened, rooted in shared experiences and mutual understanding. The fire slowly dimmed, but the warmth of their connection endured—a testament to their growing relationship and their journey together.

As the night deepened, Annie and her grandfather retired to their small cabin nestled among the trees. Inside, the soft glow of the dying embers from the campfire flickered through the window, casting gentle shadows. The soothing sound of a nearby stream, its waters murmuring against the rocks, filled the night air. They exchanged final goodnights, their voices conveying contentment and peace. In the quiet comfort of the cabin, enveloped by the tranquil sounds of nature, this adventure ended as they both drifted into a restful sleep.

On a day when the summer sun blazed overhead, Annie and her grandfather headed toward the ocean's cooling embrace. The beach stretched before them, a canvas of golden sand meeting the endless blue. The air was filled with the scent of salt and the rhythmic song of the waves.

"Feels like we could walk right into the horizon," Annie remarked, squinting against the bright sunlight.

Her grandfather chuckled, his gaze following the line where the sea kissed the sky. "The ocean has a way of putting things into perspective," he said.

They walked along the water's edge, the waves gently lapping at their feet, leaving patterns in the sand that were as transient as their living moments.

The cool water was a refreshing contrast to the day's heat, soothing their skin with every touch.

Annie thought about the ocean's vastness, its surface only hinting at the depths below. "It's like life, isn't it?" she mused. "Sometimes calm and clear, other times deep and mysterious."

Her grandfather nodded. "Life has its ebbs and flows, just like the sea. There are times of tranquility and times of turbulence. But in the end, it's all part of the same vast, beautiful experience."

They sat on the sand, watching the waves roll in and out, a never-ending cycle. The sun's warmth on their skin, the coolness of the ocean breeze, and the sound of the waves created a symphony of sensations.

"Life's like these waves," her grandfather continued. "It brings good times and bad, but what matters is how we live through each moment, the people we share it with, and the lessons we learn along the way."

Annie leaned back, letting the sand mold to her form. She felt a profound connection to the world around her, her grandfather beside her, and the lessons the ocean imparted. With its fleeting footprints and the constant ebb and flow of the tides, the beach was a reminder that life, in all its complexity, was a beautiful journey of discovery, connection, and growth.

Annie cherished these adventures, where the simplicity of nature intertwined with the complexity of their conversations. These experiences felt right, a familiar comfort in a once uncertain world. Together, she and her grandfather had found a rhythm in their lives, a harmony that resonated with their shared journey. While the pain of their past losses still lingered within them, it was now overshadowed by the joy of their newly formed family of two. Amidst this newfound peace and understanding, they planned one of their trips to Boston, a journey that promised to add another layer to their evolving relationship.

During this particular trip to the Boston hospital, the air was heavy with a mix of hope and sorrow as Annie and her grandfather made their way to her mother's room. The sight of her mother, motionless and connected to a ventilator, was a stark reminder of the fragility of life. Yet, Annie approached her with a brave smile, taking her mother's hand gently.

"Mom, I wish you could see the places Grandpa and I have been," Annie began, her voice soft but clear. "We visited the Mount Washington Hotel, the really old one in the mountains. It made me think about how every detail matters, just like in our lives."

She continued, describing their adventures with vivid details – the exhilarating climb on the Cog Railway, the profound lessons from the ocean's ebb and flow, and the deep conversations with her grandfather. "Life's like the sea, Mom. It has its depths and shallows, its calm and storms. But it's all beautiful in its own way."

As Annie spoke, she felt a faint pressure on her hand, a gentle squeeze from her mother. Her heart leaped with hope, and she glanced at the heart rate monitor, which showed a slight increase. "Mom, are you there? Can you hear me?" she asked, her voice trembling with emotion.

The doctor, entering the room, noticed the change but gently explained that it was likely just a reflex. Despite this, Annie's hope didn't wane. She continued speaking, telling her mother how much she needed her, how they were waiting for her to come home.

"Everything's okay, Mom. We're here for you. We're a family, and we're strong together. Please, come back to us," Annie whispered, her words a heartfelt plea.

In that hospital room, Annie's love and determination shone through amidst the beeps and hums of machines. She believed in her heart that her mother could hear her, that their bond was strong enough to transcend even the deepest slumber.

# Echoes of a Forgotten Past

In the tranquil cocoon Annie and her grandfather had woven around their lives, the sudden intrusion of reality came not as a thunderclap but as a chilling winter breeze. It arrived with the stern knock of the sheriff one gloomy afternoon. The Sherriff bearing a document that threatened to unravel their carefully stitched world. The claim was from Annie's biological father, a figure more myth than memory—a lumberjack from the distant woods of Northern Maine, driven not by paternal longing but by the call of financial gain.

Annie knew she was adopted, but it wasn't a topic that lingered; it was a subtle shadow, acknowledged yet unspoken. Nobody had heard from her biological father since he vanished at the first whisper of impending fatherhood. Annie's mother's high school sweetheart stood by her side through the pregnancy. They married when Annie was a baby, and he adopted her, wrapping her in his love as if she were his flesh and blood. This chapter of her past wasn't a secret; it was simply a faded memory, like a photograph left too long in the sun.

Annie's heart was a tumult of confusion. The father she had known and mourned was her dad, a man of gentle strength who had enfolded her in unconditional love. This shadow from her unremembered past sought to uproot her from the garden of peace she and her grandfather had tenderly cultivated. Her grandfather, whose years were many and whose battles were etched in the lines of his weathered face, met this new storm with a fierce, quiet determination.

With a look of sympathy poorly masked by professionalism, the sheriff handed over the documents that would shatter their tranquility. The crisp and foreboding papers declared an intent to file for full custody. It contended that Annie's biological father was not notified, nor had he consented to her adoption. Therefore, he sought legal redress to nullify the adoption, arguing that his absence in her life, though prolonged, held no legal bearing.

Annie's eyes skimmed the document, her mind struggling to piece together this legalese and paternal claims puzzle. "Grandpa, how can this be?" she asked, her voice a fragile whisper. "He left. He never wanted me. How can he just come back and claim rights now?"

Her grandfather took the papers, his hands steady despite the turmoil brewing within. "Annie, the law can be cold and blind to the matters of the heart. This man may have rights on paper, but you, my dear, have been the soul of this family. We will fight this with every ounce of strength we have."

"But I don't understand," Annie continued, tears pooling in her eyes. "Why now? Why does he want me now?"

He wrapped his arm around her, a shield against the storm. "I don't know, Annie. But remember, the roots of our family are deep, and no gust of wind, no matter how fierce, can uproot us. We are strong, you and I."

Together, they sought the counsel of a lawyer, a beacon of hope in a sea of legal uncertainties. The outcome of their struggle remained shrouded in ambiguity as letters of the law volleyed back and forth, each a harbinger of an unresolved future.

In a brazen display of entitlement, her biological father demanded immediate access to Annie, insisting on his right to take her with him. But Annie, with a courage that belied her years, stood firm, her voice resolute. "No, I don't want to see him, ever," she declared to the lawyers, her words echoing the strength she had inherited from her grandfather.

Undeterred, the biological father began a campaign of harassment, his presence a shadow that loomed over their once peaceful existence. His phone calls were like unwanted specters in the night, and his drive-bys were a constant reminder of the threat that now hung over them. Yet, in the face of this growing storm, Annie and her grandfather stood united, a fortress of two against the encroaching darkness.

Annie's biological father, a man more shadow than substance in her life, was a figure carved by the harshness of his choices and circumstances. His frame was tall and imposing, a tower of brute strength weathered by years of labor in the unforgiving forests of Northern Maine. His eyes, once perhaps bright with youthful ambition, now mirrored the bleakness of his spirit, dulled by years of solitude and the biting sting of alcohol. When he spoke, his voice was like gravel—rough and unyielding, echoing the bitterness that had taken root in his heart. All vestiges of the man he was or could have been gone, squeezed out by the darkness he created.

His presence was an unwelcome reminder of a past Annie had never known, a past that whispered of broken promises and unfulfilled responsibilities. He wore his ruggedness like armor, a shield against the world he felt had wronged him. The rare smiles that crossed his weathered face were devoid of warmth, replaced by a smirk that spoke of cynicism and unspoken grievances. This man had been hardened by life, his actions driven more by a misguided sense of entitlement than any genuine paternal affection.

The tempest reached its zenith when her biological father, fueled by a toxic brew of alcohol and avarice, darkened their doorstep. The confrontation was a clash of worlds—his volatile anger against the steadfast resolve of her grandfather, an ex-Marine whose spirit, though tempered by time, was unbroken. Her grandfather inadvertently injured the intruder in defending their sanctuary from the unwelcome encroachment across the threshold.

In the aftermath, as Annie sat beside her grandfather, their hands entwined, the weight of their predicament pressed down upon her. She reflected on their shared experiences—their resilience, the depths of their bond, and the relentless ebb and flow of life's trials. She understood, with a wisdom beyond her years, that life, like the ocean they both loved, was a cycle of highs and lows. The essence of existence lay not in avoiding storms but in the strength of the anchors one forged.

As morning dawned with a crisp awakening, yet another knock came upon their door. This time, from the local police chief, a solid and professional man that Annie's grandfather called a friend. They talked in silent whispers. Annie could only see the exasperation on the officer's face and her grandfather's steadfastness and resolve. Although she did not know the content, she surmised correctly.

"He is pressing charges," her grandfather spoke monotone, "he stated that I assaulted him."

Annie burst out, "But, he..."

"Yes, he started it, and my friend at the station is taking care of it. But it will complicate the civil case. We just have to wait and see.

As the night enveloped their home, Annie and her grandfather sat in the living room, the silence between them filled with unspoken fears and unshed tears. The house, once a sanctuary of love and memories, now felt like a fragile vessel amid a raging storm. Outside, the wind howled as if echoing their inner turmoil.

Annie gazed out the window at the old oak, her eyes reflecting the turmoil of the churning sky. "Grandpa," she whispered, her voice barely audible above the howling wind, "what if we lose? What if he takes me away?"

Her grandfather, his face a mask of tenacity lit by the flickering candlelight, took her hand in his. "Annie, life is uncertain; each moment can bring joy and pain. But remember, the strength of our bond, the love that has nurtured and sustained us, is our greatest ally. We will face this storm together, and whatever may come, we will endure. For our bond is stronger than any challenge thrown our way."

The family's equilibrium perched precariously

on a thin thread, her future uncertain and ambiguous.

# The Awakening

In the quiet of their living room, Annie and her grandfather faced the daunting reality of the legal battle. Her grandfather's voice, tinged with anger and sorrow, explained the legal complexities. "Annie, if he wins, you'll have to move with him. It's far north, a different world from here."

Annie's eyes brimmed with tears. "But Grandpa, this is my home. How can they just take me away from you?"

He sighed heavily, "The law sometimes fails to see the heart of the matter. I'll still have visitation rights, but in the winters, with the roads and the distance..."

"The snowstorms, the isolation," Annie added, her voice barely a whisper. "It's not just the distance, Grandpa. It's everything we'll lose."

They sat together, holding hands, the weight of the situation pressing down on them. The thought of being separated was unbearable, especially under such harsh conditions. The uncertainty of the upcoming court decision loomed over them, a specter of a future they both feared.

In the garden's sanctuary beneath the oak, Annie found her favorite space where time seemed to slow, where each moment lingered, heavy with emotion. She often retreated here, seeking a connection with her mother, her voice a blend of hope and desperation.

"Mom, if you can hear me, I need you," Annie whispered, her words floating on the breeze. The garden was still as if nature was listening, holding its breath. Tears traced her cheeks, the rawness of her situation pouring out.

Annie's attempts to connect with her mother grew increasingly intense. Today, it became a raw outpouring of emotion, her words steeped in desperation and longing.

"Mom, please, I need you," Annie cried out, her voice breaking under the weight of her emotions. Her plea was more than a call; it was a heartfelt cry transcending the physical realm, reaching out to the ethereal space where her mother lingered.

This surge of raw emotion was the key. It bridged the vast expanse between them, and at that moment, something happened. As time stopped, the world around her became silent. The birds held their singing, the wind perfectly still, and the forest hushed to an eerie silence.

Then, in that lingering quiet, a whisper brushed her consciousness, faint yet unmistakable. "Annie," her mother's ethereal voice seemed to echo from a distant place. Startled, Annie's heart raced. "Mom, is that you?"

"I hear you," her mother's voice, quieter than the flutter of a butterfly's wings, "I'm trying to find you."

"I'm here, mom. I'm right here..." Annie crumbled to all fours, tears pooling between the dancing green grass, "Mom."

As they communicated, it felt like Annie was

reaching across a vast expanse, her words a bridge to the ethereal realm where her mother resided. The conversation was fragmented, like a dream half-remembered. Annie spoke of the custody battle, of her fears and longings. Her mother's voice, though distant, was filled with warmth and understanding. "I am here, Annie. Keep talking to me. Keep showing me the way."

Days passed, each marked by these ethereal conversations. This newfound level of communication, though emotionally exhausting for Annie, was a beacon of hope, a sign that her mother was fighting to return to the world they once shared.

Then, one morning, a phone call came from the hospital. There was a change in her mother's condition, subtle yet significant. The doctors couldn't explain it, but Annie knew. Their connection and their conversations were making a difference. This glimmer of hope, faint as it was, fortified Annie's resolve. She would continue to be the guiding light, leading her mother back from the brink to the world of the living.

The dawn barely broke when Annie and her grandfather set out for Boston, a sense of urgency propelling them forward. The old pickup truck rumbled down the highway, each mile bringing them closer to the hospital to Annie's mother.

Arriving at the hospital, Annie barely waited for the truck to stop before she was out the door, her grandfather close behind. They navigated the hospital's sterile corridors with a singular focus, reaching her mother's room with hearts pounding.

Inside, the room was bathed in soft morning light. Annie approached her mother's bedside, taking her hand gently. "Mom, it's me, Annie. Please, come back to us," she pleaded, her voice thick with emotion.

For a moment, there was only the sound of the machines, the steady beep of the heart monitor. Then, subtly, her mother's lips quivered, a faint murmur escaping them. Her eyelids fluttered, a sign of the struggle within.

"Mom, I need you. We need you. Please, fight your way back," Annie urged, tears streaming down her cheeks. "We've been talking under the oak tree. I've been telling you everything. I know you can hear me."

Her grandfather stood by, his eyes glistening with unspoken hope. The room felt charged with a palpable energy, a connection transcending consciousness's boundaries.

A tender, miraculous moment unfolded in the hushed room as Annie and her grandfather kept their watchful vigil. Her mother's lips quivered, and a faint but unmistakably clear "Annie" resonated through the room, a whisper laden with a thousand emotions. The nurse, who had been a silent, watchful presence, suddenly sprang to life; welling in tears, she rushed out to call the doctor, her movements a blur of urgency.

Annie, overcome with a torrent of emotions, collapsed beside her mother, her embrace a fusion of joy, relief, and profound love. "I knew you could hear me, Mom. I knew you'd find your way back," she cried, her voice a symphony of tears and laughter, each word a testament to their unbreakable bond.

The doctor's arrival brought a flurry of activity. As she checked the vitals and scrutinized the instruments, her eyes reflected a mix of professional skepticism and genuine wonder. Turning to Annie, her voice softened, "You are one special young lady."

Once a place of somber watch, the room was now alive with a restrained hope. Annie and her grandfather stayed close to the bedside, each moment more precious than the last. The fading daylight signaled the end of visiting hours. They reluctantly left the room that evening, their hearts brimming with a notion so profound it defied words, a feeling that lingered long after the hospital lights dimmed.

Annie's heart was filled with hope and apprehension as they left the hospital. The subtle responses from her mother were like rays of light piercing the darkness of her coma. This was a sign, a glimmer of hope that her mother was still fighting, still present, and that their bond was a lifeline pulling her back from the abyss.

The days that followed were tinted with a blend of hope and sorrow. Annie clung to the subtle signs of her mother's awakening, but the shadow of the court case loomed large.

The day of the hearing dawned bleak and heavy-hearted.

"It's time to go," Annie's grandfather said with a penetrating seriousness. Annie looked down and took a step back, "no."

Her grandfather reached out his hand, "Have faith, little one. It's time."

They arrived. The courthouse stood imposing and sterile, its stark, corporate structure a sharp contrast to the warmth of Annie's home and the welcoming garden. As Annie ascended the courthouse stairs, each step was measured cautiously. Her hand, nestled within her grandfather's, trembled subtly, betraying her inner turmoil. The uncertainty in her eyes and the slight falter in her stride all spoke of her reluctance to enter a place where her fate hung in the balance.

The heavy door to the courtroom creaked open, revealing a world of cold formality. Inside, the room was intimidating, with rows of wooden benches and the judge's seat looming authoritatively above. Annie hesitated before sitting, sandwiched between her grandfather and their lawyer. She scanned the room, her heart pounding.

Her eyes settled on her biological father at the opposite table. A man unfamiliar. He appeared disheveled, his indifference palpable even from a distance. Seeing him stirred a mix of emotions in Annie - confusion, anger, a sense of injustice.

The proceedings began, and Annie felt dwarfed by the grandeur and severity of the courtroom. The judge's voice echoed, each word amplifying her anxiety. As the reality of the situation sank in, a sense of helplessness enveloped her, leaving her feeling small and vulnerable in the vast, impersonal room.

The judge delivered a verdict that reverberated through their souls – temporary custody was granted to Annie's biological father. The possibility of it becoming permanent hung like a grim specter.

Annie's world seemed to collapse as the judge's words fell like hammer blows. She crumpled under the weight of disbelief and fear. Her eyes clouded with despair; she clung to her grandfather's side, a lifeline in the tumultuous sea terrorizing disbelief.

Annie's grandfather, the unwavering rock in her life, was a picture of profound sorrow. The stoicism that had always been his armor was now pierced, revealing a depth of vulnerability that was heartbreakingly rare. His eyes, which had always danced with vitality and wisdom, now mirrored the storm of loss and uncertainty that loomed ahead.

The journey home was silent. Annie, her eyes a window to her fractured world, gazed out at the blur of scenery, each mile a step further from the life she knew. Her grandfather, steady on the wheel, drove with a hollow precision. The car, a sanctuary of their shared anguish, moved through the world as a vessel of their unspoken grief. Words were redundant in this space; their heavy hearts resonated with a language of pain and unyielding love, filling the void with a poignant, unarticulated understanding.

The morning of the custody transfer was a day heavy with foreboding. Annie's biological father arrived, law enforcement in tow, his intentions unmistakable. In a desperate bid for freedom, Annie dashed to the garden, her sanctuary under the oak tree. Her tears carved rivers down her cheeks as she scrambled into the low branches. Her heart shattered at the thought of being torn from the life she loved.

The duty-bound yet empathetic sheriff followed her, his calls for her to emerge echoing through the garden. Her grandfather, his voice laced with desperation, pleaded for understanding, but his words fell on deaf ears. The biological father, gruff and impatient, dismissed him with disdain.

As the confrontation escalated beneath the oak, Annie, hidden within its branches, tried to climb higher, away from the unfolding nightmare. Suddenly, a coarse hand grasped her leg, yanking her downwards. Annie screamed as her grandfather lunged forward to intervene. But the sheriff's stern warning halted him.

Engulfed in her biological father's unwelcome embrace, Annie fought fiercely, her small frame writhing in an attempt to escape. Her screams, laden with raw fear and desperation, tore through the morning air, a stark, heart-wrenching sound that echoed off the garden walls. Each cry of "No!" was a plea, a testament to her struggle, resonating with the pain of being torn from the life and love she knew. Her arms flailed, seeking freedom, as tears blurred her vision, each drop a symbol of her profound anguish and unyielding spirit in the face of this harrowing ordeal.

Amidst this chaos, a commanding voice pierced through the tension. "What the hell is going on here? Put her down now!"

They turned to see an astonishing sight – Annie's mother, frail yet fierce, her presence electrifying. The police chief supported her gently, his stance protective.

Annie kicked furiously, releasing herself from the unwanted bonds. She sprinted towards her mother. Her biological father stepped forward to grab her, but in a swift, violent motion, her grandfather tackled the man to the ground, ensuring Annie's unimpeded path to safety.

The police chief's firm declaration, "It's over. Time for you to leave," was echoed by the sheriff's stern command, "Now." The two men formed a wall and ushered him away. Defeated and fuming, the biological father retreated, his threats of return hanging hollowly in the air.

The reunion of mother and daughter was a poignant blend of tears and relief, a moment of profound triumph. Annie and her mother locked in an embrace under the oak tree, a symbol of their enduring strength. Her grandfather, overwhelmed with relief, watched on his knees, a silent prayer of gratitude on his lips. The turmoil had ended, their bond unbroken, under the watchful boughs of the old oak tree.

# Girl in the Sun

The sunlight danced through the leaves, casting a kaleidoscope of light and shadow. The old oak stood witness to a heartwarming scene. A woman, hair graced with strands of silver, stood by the swing that hung from a sturdy branch. Her hands gently pushed a small girl whose bright, joyful laughter rang through the air. The child's laughter, a melody unique and new. The aged woman—familiar yet different. The scene itself held a curiosity.

Much time had passed since the turmoil of the custody battle. Annie's biological father faded into a distant memory, allowing Annie and her mother to rekindle and build a life of love and stability. The garden flourished, and the oak continued its watch over the land and the family.

Leaping from the swing, the girl ran playfully around the tree. "Catch me, Grandma. Catch me," she quipped. The woman's laughter reverberated and carried across the fields. Annie smiled. She looked on, watching her daughter and mother play. Her husband gently held her hand.

Annie had flourished after her mother returned. She went to college and became a teacher. She found love and embraced the joys of motherhood. Her husband, a compassionate doctor, has become a cornerstone of the family and their small community. The loss of her grandfather, a poignant chapter in their lives, brought sorrow but also a deeper appreciation for the time they had together. He rests peacefully beside his wife in the family cemetery, a serene place where the fields meet the forest. On certain days, when the sun's tentacled reach is perfect, the light bounces off the marble gravestones, sending sparkling flickers of iridescent light in all directions. "Hi, Grandpa," Annie would say softly.

It was on a Summer Solstice. The midday sun

bathed the garden in a radiant glow. The massive oak, a sentinel of time, stood tall as Annie observed her daughter, Harmony, and her mother by its base. At its zenith, the sun showered them in golden light, painting the scene with an almost ethereal quality. Baking in the sun's warmth, Harmony looked up with innocent eyes and giggled, "The tree is talking to me." This simple declaration held profound meaning, a testament to the gift passed down through generations. Watching this beautiful exchange, Annie felt a deep connection to her roots and the natural world around her. Their family's legacy, intertwined with nature's spiritual energy, was now flourishing in Harmony. At that moment, under the oak tree, enveloped in the luminous embrace of the sun, the continuity of their bond was evident. The legacy of the girl in the sun continued, strong and enduring.

*The End*

www.ingramcontent.com/pod-product-compliance
Lightning Source LLC
Chambersburg PA
CBHW042033120726

47911CB00026B/723